Nose to Toes

For my parents, who gave me the gift of childhood
– M. B.

To my good friend Annie Thibault, for your help and support
– M. S.

A big thank-you to president and publisher Sheba Meland and editor Anne Shone, both of Owl Books, and to Kat Mototsune, for their expertise and enthusiasm. A special thank-you to Marisol Sarrazin for her engaging illustrations, which bring magic to the book. – M. B.

Text copyright © 2001 by Marilyn Baillie
Illustrations copyright © 2001 by Marisol Sarrazin

Published by Caroline House
Boyds Mills Press, Inc.
A Highlights Company
815 Church Street
Honesdale, Pennsylvania 18431
Printed in Hong Kong

Published simultaneously in Canada by Owl Books
51 Front Street East, Suite 200
Toronto, Ontario M5E 1B3

U.S. Cataloging-in-Publication Data
    (Library of Congress Standards)

Baillie, Marilyn.
    Nose to toes / by Marilyn Baillie ; illustrations by Marisol Sarrazin. —1st ed.
  [32] p. : col. ill. ;   cm.
  Summary: A look at all the amazing ways a child's body can work and move.
  ISBN 1-56397-319-7
  1. Musculoskeletal system. 2. Human locomotion. I. Sarrazin, Marisol. II. Title.
    612.7/ 6 21 2001 CIP AC
Library of Congress Catalog Card Number 00-109372

First edition, 2001
Book designed by Word and Image Design Studio
The text of this book is set in 24-point Meridien Medium.

Visit us on the World Wide Web at www.boydsmillspress.com

10 9 8 7 6 5 4 3 2 1

Nose to Toes

Marilyn Baillie
Illustrated by Marisol Sarrazin

BOYDS MILLS PRESS

My head and feet,
my hands and toes,
eyes, ears, mouth, and nose . . .
My body does amazing things.

My hands can hold and squeeze.
My legs can jump and run.
My mouth can sip and slurp.

And when I close my eyes I can pretend . . .
to be most anything!

I can be a turtle, and pull my head inside.

But then — peek-a-boo — I can poke it out, too!

When I'm a cat, I go hunting at night.
The shine in my eyes
helps me see in dim light.

I am a dog, and I hear you call my name.

My ears move around,
catching sounds from far away.

I'm a hungry little lamb sniffing a treat.

My nose lets me know
exactly where to go.

Pull, pull, tug! I'm a robin and
my mouth is a beak.

When I find a yummy worm,
I slurp it up to eat.

I'm a sleepy, snoozy lion cub,
safe with my mother.

We snuggle close and with our arms
we hug each other.

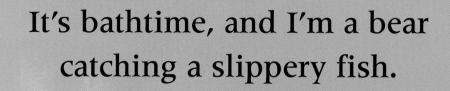

It's bathtime, and I'm a bear
catching a slippery fish.

I grab it with my great big hands.
Oops! Kersplish!

My tiny mouse fingers
hold on tight . . .

to my big, sweet treat to eat.
Yum, slurp, bite!

I'm a kangaroo jumping
with my long, strong legs.

Short hops and long leaps
take me up, up, and away!

Splish, splash! I'm a duck with big, flat feet.

When I swim, they're like paddles.
But on land, I just waddle.

At playtime I'm a chimpanzee,
hanging on with my toes.

We push and pull, my friend and I.
Whose toes are those?

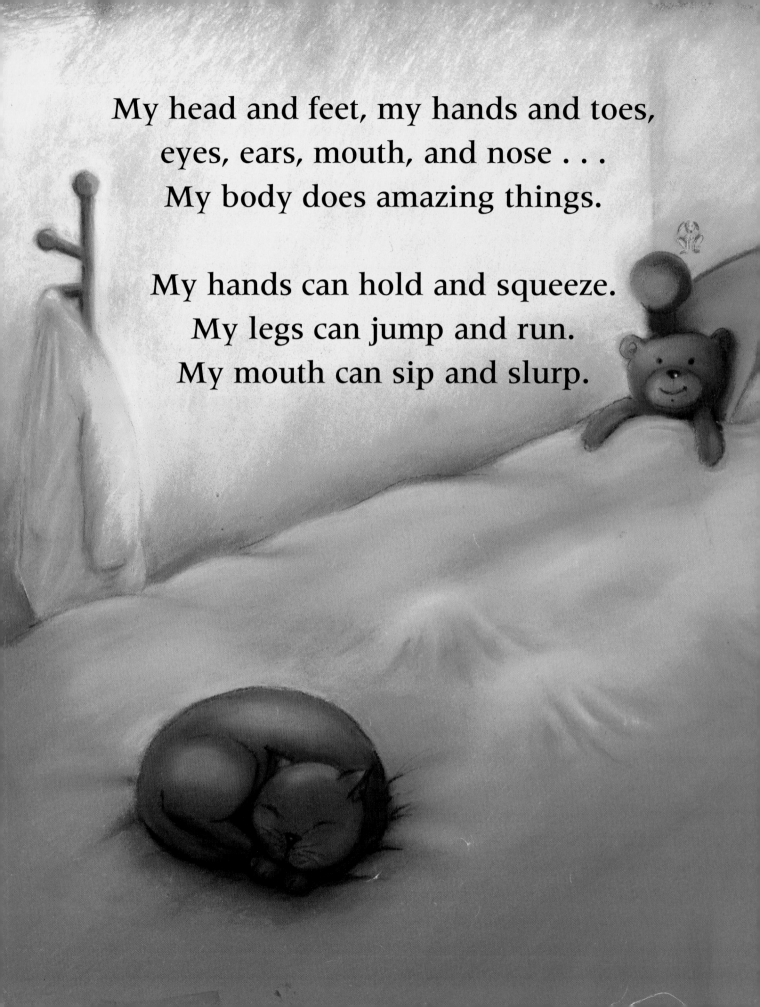

My head and feet, my hands and toes,
eyes, ears, mouth, and nose . . .
My body does amazing things.

My hands can hold and squeeze.
My legs can jump and run.
My mouth can sip and slurp.

And when I curl up and go to sleep
I'm glad to be just me!

Guess What?

TURTLES carry a big roof over their heads. Their shell is a hideout, a home, a hard roof, and a sun umbrella.

Why do **CATS** have shiny eyes at night? Bright areas at the back of their eyes are like mirrors. This helps their eyes to catch more light.

DOGS often prick up their ears. Their ears are catching sounds from so far away that you can't even hear the noises.

LAMBS know with their noses. In a large flock of sheep, babies and moms find each other by smell and by sound.

ROBINS can build with their beaks. They carry twigs, grass, and mud in their beaks to a safe nesting place. Then their busy beaks work fast to form a cozy nest.

LION cubs love to play. Cubs tumble and tease and pounce on each other. Soon they will learn to hunt and pounce with their strong front legs and catch their supper.

Grizzly **BEARS** aren't fussy eaters. They use their paws to fish for fish, pick fruit and berries, dig up roots, and catch other animals.

A **MOUSE** in your house is hard to hear. Mice have rubbery pads on their paws so they can silently sneak about.

Don't race with a **KANGAROO**! A large kangaroo can go as fast as a car in the city. It can also leap over bushes and fences and swim across streams.

Mallard **DUCKS** are great swimmers! Their feet are wide and webbed to help push them through the water. Their bodies are light and shaped to travel; their feathers keep them warm and dry.

Do **CHIMPANZEES** have thumbs on their feet? The big toe on a chimpanzee's foot works like your thumb. Its other toes are more like your fingers. Their toes can grasp, hold, grip, and climb.

Join the Fun!

Crouch down like a tiny mouse. Stretch up tall like a big, furry bear. Flip-flop your feet and wiggle-waddle to and fro. In the blink of an eye, you're a duck in a pond, you're a mouse in a house, you're a bear in a lair. As you turn from page to page, join in to see what wonderful animal you can be. From nose to toes, animals use their bodies in amazing ways.

Who has special eyes to see in the night? Who has thumbs for toes to swing high in trees? Who hides its head under its own umbrella to stay in the shade? Now try to see what you can do. You'll find out that your body works in amazing ways, too!

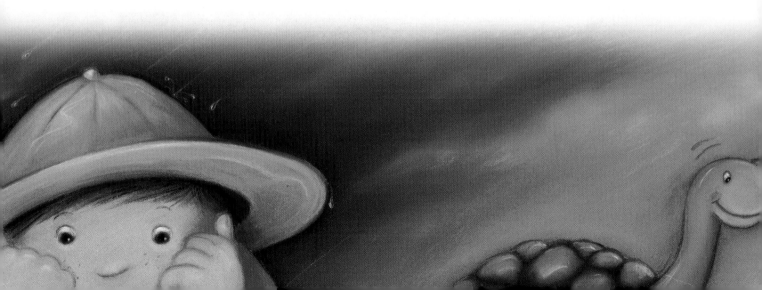